PRINCESS PINKY AND CAT LARSON.

PART 4.

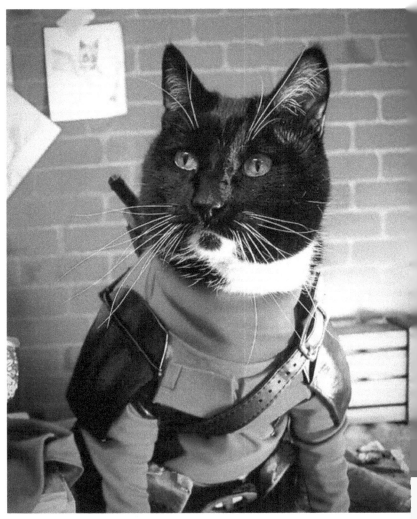

EMILY'S SECRET VISIT TO THE WITCHES PARTY.
GABRIELL MONRO
GABRIELL MONRO

PART 4

PROLOGUE

In the 3rd book, Emily flies on the Unicorn to the Magic Kingdom of the Darkness to save her sister Nelly. She tried to fight against the magic power which turned Nelly into a witch.

Emily goes through a lot of secret adventures on her way, but she always has her faithful Cat Larson by her side.

Princess Pinky gets in trouble again and Emily is going to help her.

Emily was fast asleep dreaming of her new friends in the secret Magical Kingdom of Wampadoo. Cat Larson was sleeping on Emily's bed right next to Emily's head, keeping them warm.

Oh, what fun Emily had with her friends. She was dreaming about her next adventure when in her dream Princess Pinky called her to come quickly.

There was trouble in Wampadoo and Emily and cat Larson were needed urgently.

Emily woke up instantly. She looked around her small bedroom. Everything was the same as it was when she went to sleep.

She was asking herself if she was dreaming or did Princess Pinky call her. She woke cat Larson, who stretched like all cats do when they wake up from sleeping.

He looked at Emily and said: "What's wrong Emily, why have we woken up when it is still dark?"

"I think, Princess Pinky is in trouble and needs us there as fast as we can go" said Emily.

Cat Larson asked again: "So what's wrong?"

Emily replied: "I'm not sure, but we better go quickly."

Without a second to waste, Cat Larson held Emily's hand. In the blink of an eye, they were both standing outside of the Palace gates.

An Orange Giraffe was looking over the wall, waiting for them to arrive.

As soon as he saw them, he called down the Green Elephant to sound his trumpet to let Princess Pinky know, that they had come.

Princess Pinky came quickly: "I'm so pleased you could both come. We have a problem and I disparately need your help."

Princess Pinky thanked the orange Giraffe and the Green Elephant for their help.

She turned around to Emily and Cat Larson: "This way, Quickly. When we are inside the Castle I will tell you all about it."

They ran into the safety of the Castle and the giant doors slammed closed behind them with a loud crash.

Princess Pinky could hardly get her words out. She was out of breath and very troubled.

"We have a problem," she said.

"The wicked Witch Wilella is having a Witches Coven. All of the wicked witches from the Dark Witches Magic Kingdom will be there".

Then Princess Pinky looked at Emily and saw, that she was waiting for her explanation. She could not even imagine, that it was dangerous for everybody.

"Prince Louis has told me all about the Witches Coven and how they plan to make lots of trouble for everyone,"

continued Princess Pinky.

Emily was surprised by this. She had never seen a Witches Coven.

She was wondering, what it would be like. What would they look like, were they young or old?

What colour hair did they have and how would they get there?

Would they be flying on their broomsticks or magic carpets?

Larson tugged Emily on the arm: "What are you thinking about?"

"Oh. Nothing," Emily replied.

Princess Pinky explained to them:

"We need to go to Wilella's Castle and see what they are doing."

The way to the Witches' Castle was a dangerous one with many difficult paths to take. They would have to go through the Pirates' Forest.

They will go across the high mountains with snow on top of them.

Then the trip will be through the woods where the snakes were, a very difficult journey indeed.

"We don't have much time and we need to go now," asked Princess Pinky.

Emily replied: "How are we going to get there?"

Princess Pinky said: "We will go on the Unicorn's back.

He will carry all of us. Then if we can not go far, we will go on the Dragon's back. He can fly us there."

Emily wanted to ask a question which was bothering her for a while:

"What will we do, when we get there?"

Princess Pinky replied: "We need to see what they are up to and stop them from causing trouble."

So the journey began. They climbed onto the Unicorn.

"Hold on tight," Princess Pinky warned everybody.

The Dragon was following behind, making sure that they were not followed.

The Witch Wilella had spies at Princess Pinky's Castle, but Princess Pinky didn't know who they were.

She believed that everyone in the castle was her friend and that nobody would tell the witch anything. But Princess Pinky had a little problem in her magic Castle, but how could she find out who it was?

They came to the Pirates' forest. It was dark and creepy. The grass was tall and the wind whistled through the leaves on the trees. It was very creepy.

Emily warned her friends: "We better be quiet and not make a sound or the Pirates will catch us."

As they came towards the Pirates village, pirate Sam was in the watch tower. It was swaying from side to side in the heavy wind.

This made Sam feel a little seasick, but he had a job to do. No one ever came past the pirates' village. Most of the pirates were sleeping after their party, which had lots of food and drink.

They were tired and sleepy. Sam didn't see the Unicorn with Emily and her friends go past. They were very quiet and didn't make a sound.

Now it was on towards the mountains and cross over the snow on top of the mountains.

No one from the party saw the 2 crows flying over them. The crows were the spies for Wilella.

They were going to tell Wilella, that Princess Pinky and Emily were on their way to the Witches' Castle.

Now at the Witches Castle, Wilella was welcoming her friends, the other witches from the Dark Magic Kingdom.

They were going to have their party and have lots of food, ice cream and jelly and cakes and bottles of pop to drink.

One by one the other witches arrived. They parked their broomsticks by the door and went in, in front of them was a table full of food, cakes and fizzy pop and ice cream and jelly.

They were going to have a great party before going to bed. In the morning, they were going to have the Coven.

It would be around a big cauldron, which was on top of a fire, this cauldron was used on Wilella's special occasions. This is where Wilella and the other witches would cast their spells and make their potions.

These were potions that were used to turn people into frogs, hamsters and other small creatures if they had upset Wilella.

It wasn't long before the crows arrived at Wilella's castle. They carried the news Wilella had been waiting for a long time.

Princess Pinky, Cat Larson and Emily were on their way to the Witches' Castle.

Wilella took out her crystal ball, waving her hands over the crystal ball she cleared the clouds inside the crystal ball to see everything.

"They are close to the mountains, but why didn't the pirates see then?" she asked.

The other witches shook their heads, they were too busy looking into the crystal ball.

"We will have to keep a close eye on where they are, just so we can prepare a little surprise for them," Wilella explained her plan to the other witches.

The witch from the South of the Dark Magic Kingdom asked suddenly: "What will that be?"

Wilella replied to her: "We will have to think about that."

Emily and her friends were close to the mountains. They looked up and they could see the snow on the top.

Emily was thinking, that looks very cold up there, but we have to cross them to get to the Witches Castle.

Before long they were coming to the top, it was cold but not as cold as Emily had thought it would.

Cat Larson was lying around Emily's neck his fur was keeping her warm.

They were at the bottom of the mountains soon and following the path towards the wood of snakes.

Along the path close to some trees the King Snake, a Cobra was wrapped around a branch. He hissed as the group came close:

"You need to tell me the secret word to go by and it will keep you safe". Princess Pinky wasn't sure what it was. She had to think fast, so they could carry on to Wilella's Castle. But what is it she thought?

Then it came to her, she said in a polite voice, the Cobra is King. After all, he was a King Cobra.

He hissed, that's correct you may pass now, but be quick as the other snakes will soon be awake.

Soon they passed the wood, in front of them was Wilella's Castle. They could hear the party taking place.

There was lots of singing and music coming from the hall, they could see a big party through the windows and the witches dancing.

Emily asked her friends: "How are we going to go into the Castle?"

Then the Dragon replied: "We can enter by the secret door. It was around the back and under an arch close to the moat where the blue octopus lives. I've been in that way before."

"Are there any traps?" Emily was still worried about this plan.

"I don't think so", answered the Dragon to make her feel calmer. They quickly and quietly went to the back of the castle.

Princess Pinky, Emily and Cat Larson found the entrance. When the friends went inside, they left the Unicorn on watch with instructions that if anything happened to them, he was to get help as fast as he could.

The entrance was dark and covered in cobwebs.

They were hanging from the ceiling and walls. It was damp and smelly. This was not used very often and the witch had forgotten all about it.

They came to the end of the tunnel. In front of them was a small door. They were wondering, how they would get through to the other of the side as they were too big to go through the door.

Then Princess Pinky explained: "We are in the Dark Magic Kingdom.

We can shrink down to the size of the door to go in the room behind the door."

Instantly they shrunk, went through the door and into the room on the other side. As soon as everybody was in the room they went back to their normal size.

Emily thought this was great fun and she could play lots of tricks on her sister if she could shrink and return to her normal size.

Cat Larson said: "We have to wait until the witches are asleep after their party and then we can see what they are planning".

Soon it was light, they had travelled all night and Emily was too excited to feel sleepy.

She knew that they had to stop the witches, but first they needed to know what the witches were planning.

They crept around very quietly so as not to wake up the witches. They came to the special room, where Wilella had her big cauldron over the fire. The cauldron that Wilella cooked her potions in.

Princess Pinky whispered: "We need to empty the cauldron and make it so it doesn't work any more.

They waited till the fire was out and the cauldron had cooled down. They lifted it and turned onto its side, all the potion inside spilt all over the floor.

It wet Emily's feet, her socks and shoes were wet. However, funny things started to happen, her feet started to grow and her socks ripped.

Her toes poked out of the end of her shoes. Emily was worried as they were her best shoes and her mummy would not be very pleased as they had cost a lot of money.

Princess Pinky told her not to worry has everything would return to normal when they reached Princess Pinky's Castle.

The dragon who was holding the big pot dropped it on the floor.

It smashed into a thousand pieces, the noise woke up the witches and now it was a race to leave the castle.

The friends quickly went back the way they had come, only this time one of Wilella's guards was blocking the door, the small door that led to the tunnel.

The guard was a very big spider. He was the magic creature, that was the leader of the spider army, which protected Wilella's Castle.

They had been caught and Wilella was angry, her best magic cauldron was broken.

The spider took them to the castle dungeons. The door slammed behind them. It was dark and cold and the friends were wondering how they could tell the Unicorn to go for help.

They were waiting but did not have to wait very long.

Wilella stood in the doorway. Her face was red with anger.

Steam was coming from her ears, she stamped hard on the ground. Her foot went through the floor which made her even madder.

It was while Wilella's foot was stuck in the floor that the friends escaped, they rushed past knocking Wilella over.

They ran out of the dungeon and down the corridor to the room with the small door, just like before they all shrank down so they could go through.

Once on the other side, they returned to their normal size, they quickly went down the cold, cobwebbed corridor and out into the light.

They can see waiting for them was the Unicorn, ready to make their retreat back to Princess Pinky's Castle.

Wilella's Castle was very noisy with lots of shouting from all the witches as they were disappointed that their weekend had been spoiled.

The friends' journey home was the way they had come but it was backwards.

First, they had to get past the wood with the snakes and climb the mountains, then on past the pirates.

They came to the wood. Then they stopped and listened. they couldn't hear any hisses, where were the snakes, it was quiet.

The friends moved slowly but quietly and then from the top of a tree the King Cobra swung down. He hissed to them:

"Where do you think you are going?"

It was quiet for a few seconds, then Princess Pinky remembered the secret word.

She said it so they could all hear "The Cobra is King".

The snake moved a little upwards. He hissed and then said:

"I will let you pass, but I need you to send me some cakes and ice cream so we snakes can have a party."

The Princess was very happy to send cakes and ice cream to the snakes and told the King Cobra it would be done as soon as they were back in Princess Pinky's Castle.

The group of friends continued on their path to the mountains. They could see the snow was still on top. Emily thought about the journey the other way.

Cat Larson was standing close to her, he whispered to her, "don't worry about the cold I will wrap myself around you and keep you warm".

Soon he jumped onto Emily's shoulders wrapping himself around Emily.

They were warm over the top of the mountain and down the other side to the path that would take them to the Pirates' forest.

The friends continued on their way, moving as quickly and quietly as they could. However, in front of them was the pirates.

They had to go past the village, past the watch tower. It was still windy and the crows' nest was still swaying from side to side, but not as much as before.

Pirate Sam was still in his place, still feeling seasick from all the movement, side to side.

Below the pirates were still in bed after their all night party. Once again Sam didn't see the friends go past. They were quickly out of the forest and close to Princess Pinky's Castle.

The Orange Giraffe was quick to see them, he lent over and whispered into the green elephant's ear:

"The Princess and her friends are back. Let everyone know that they are safe."

Without a second to waste, the elephant lifted this trunk and trumpeted with excitement that they were all home.

The draw bridge was lowered and the friends crossed into the Castle.

The witches had been fooled again and it was done by Princess Pinky with her best friend Emily. Cat Larson was there in a quiet sort of way.

He was the one with the magic that made them small and then tall.

Larson looked at Emily and said: "I think it is time we went back."

Emily looked sad as she liked being there, but time was time and it was time to go home.

She did not know at that time, that Witch Wilella prepared a trap for her and her friends on the way back.

Emily said "Goodbye" to Princess Pinky and other friends in the Castle and jumped on the neck of the Unicorn. Cat Larson was behind her as he did not like flying like every cat.

The Unicorn left the ground in a second, but suddenly he was surrounded by the group of witches which were sent by Wilella.

They shout very loudly and tried to use the magic spells of the witches to turn the Unicorn into a lizard. The vicious power started to work in the beginning.

The Unicorn's tail changed to a lizard's tail, which put Emily and Cat Larson in distress.

They can't imagine what would happen to all of them in a few minutes when they will fall from the Unicorn during the flight in the air.

Suddenly, they heard a scream from one of the witches. They turn their heads in that direction where they heard the noise and saw the Magic Red Dragon approaching them.

Cat Larson grabbed Emily's hand and explained:

"We are saved. Princess Pinky sent her best security guard, Magic Red Dragon, to help us. He will protect us from these wicked witches during our back trip".

Emily was happy to hear this. She was looking at the crazy witches, who were trying to escape from the fire over their heads.

Magic Red Dragon was chasing the witches in the air. Their broomsticks were slow enough for them to be caught.

The battle was over in a few minutes.

Two witches escaped and fled back to Wilella's Castle to tell her about the failure of her cunning plan.

The Unicorn with Emily and Cat Larson landed in the middle of a sunflower's field to have a rest.

Emily wanted to thank the Magic Red Dragon for saving them. He approached them from a short distance to see, if they were fine.

He looked huge and when Emily came to him, she can see only his big feet. The Magic Red Dragon lowered down his head and looked at Emily with his shiny eyes.

Emily had never seen such a huge dragon so close to her. If she wants to, she can move her hand and touch his nose and his head.

He looked even pretty now as he was pleased with the attention and his saving mission.

"Thank you for your help. You saved us from Wilella's witches and we are very grateful to you", said Emily to the Red Dragon.

"I was sent to help you by Princess Pinky and I could see that I arrived in time.

We knew, that Wilella was very angry after her Witches' Party and she will try to pay you back", said Magic Red Dragon.

The Unicorn and Cat Larson were listening to their conversation not far from them.

Suddenly, Cat Larson saw a beautiful lizard not far from him. The lizard was looking at the Unicorn's new tail as he had a lizard tail now.

Then the lizard disappeared somewhere in an unknown direction for a few seconds. Then she came back with the small lilac flower in her mouth.

She approached the Unicorn and showed him that he needed to eat this flower. Then she pointed again at his lizard's tail.

Emily guessed what it means:

"I think, this unusual lizard is asking you to eat this magic flower, which she brought for you.

Hopefully, it will overcome the witches' magic and your tail will be back to normal".

She was right about this. As soon as Unicorn swallowed the special flower, his tail changed again to his usual one.

It was a miracle, which Emily had never seen before. She was thinking now:

"Well... There is too much magic around. I need to be careful even with the flowers. You never know, what can turn you into a rat or which flower can help you".

The secret lizard disappeared as quickly as it was possible to see it. Everybody was thinking that their dangerous trip was almost over, but they were wrong.

Suddenly, Cat Larson looked at the end of the field and saw the strange 6 stones, which were standing up all in different shapes.

The most amazing thing was that the stones were changing their colours. They became blue, then red, then green then blue again.

This was very unusual and the group of friends decided to come close to see, what was going on there.

When they stepped close to this exotic place, strange thoughts appeared in Emily's head. She read somewhere in the past about the Magic Stones of Galaxy.

Most people had never seen them at all in their life. However, if somebody was lucky enough to find this place, they can ask these Magic Stones for 3 wishes.

On the other side, it needed to be very careful with what you wished for. One person who found these stones before turned to the ball.

He just wish to be easy going all the time, but the Magic Stones granted his wish in a very strange way.

It was unclear, how that story ended, was it a lucky one or a sad one?

Cat Larson looked at Emily and he saw, that she was in doubt. He held her arm and said:

"I know what you are thinking about. If you do not want, you don't need to make any wishes and try the luck of the magic. Just everything leave it like it is".

Emily did not know, what to say to him. She saw that the Magic Red Dragon approached the Magic Stones of Galaxy first. Then he touched the nearest stone and made the wish.

What happened next was a big surprise for everybody.

Suddenly, the big Red Dragon turned into the little smiley Baby Dragon, how he looked many years ago.

"Oh. What we will be doing with this baby?" asked Emily.

"We need to return him back to his adulthood. Let's ask him to touch another stone. Maybe it will help", replied Cat Larson. He brought the Baby Dragon to the next

Magic Stone and placed his arm over the top of it.

This action worked, but in the wrong way again. The Baby Dragon turn into the beautiful White Fox.

His lovely fur was so shiny and soft, that everybody had the great desire to touch him and hug him.

White Fox looked at Emily and her friends and said to them in a gentle voice:

"I like my new appearance, but my grandmother will not recognize me. We had never had foxes before among our relatives.

I had a feeling, that Magic Stones work in the opposite way".

"What do you mean?" asked him Emily. She was ready to agree with the White Fox.

It looks like every wish from the Magic Stones turns the wrong way from the beginning.

Cat Larson joined their conversation and explained:

"I think, I know the magic of these stones. They work the opposite way.

They turn you into somebody or something, which you want to be in your early childhood.

However, if we guess right about this magic, it will lose its power. Everything will be back as usual.

Let's try the last Magic Stone with the bright Blue Light inside of it. I hope it will work in the end".

Cat Larson asked White Fox to touch the stone, which he choose for him. The miracle happened in the next few seconds in front of their eyes.

White Fox started to change his colours. Then it turned to the little Red Dragon, who started to grow to his normal size within a minute.

When Emily looked at the Red Dragon again, she can see his big feet, which were standing in front of her.

She realised, that the miracle worked and the Magic Stones lost their power over them.

The Red Dragon looked happy to be back to his normal appearance.

He fled back to the Castle to tell his grandmother and his family the secret story about his changes and adventures.

Meanwhile, Cat Larson looked at Emily and asked her:

"Do you want to try your good luck and touch that little Small Magic Stone which is located far from the group of other stones?

I have a feeling, that it will work in a different magic way".

Emily thought for a few minutes and said:

"Yes. I wished to have the most amazing beautiful dress, which I wanted to have from my childhood. It will be very light and you can not feel any weight of it.

I would like, that it will change the colours with the sun- rise and sunset. I don't think, I asked too much?" said Emily to Cat Larson.

"No. You are not. Do not worry about it, just touch this special stone. It's just waiting for you".

Emily followed his advice and placed her little hand over the top of the strange stone. She felt the warmth, which was coming from it and she closed her eyes for a second.

When she opened her eyes again and looked at herself, she can see the most amazing dress she ever saw.

Two white swans were flying in front of her and they held the dress of her dreams in their beaks.

Emily's children's dream had came true and she was dressed in the most beautiful magic outfit she could ever wish for.

She felt like a princess and then she suddenly realised, that it was happening with her and nobody else.

Cat Larson and the Unicorn looked at her and admired how she looked.

"You have a gold heart and you deserved to be spoiled", said Cat Larson to Emily.

The Unicorn agreed with her and replied:

"You are always ready to help your friends and you are the bravest girl I have ever met".

Emily was very happy to hear these comments from her friends. It looked like her adventure was going a nice way.

However, it was the right time to think about the way back home.

Cat Larson held Emily's hand and just as the adventure had started it was over, a puff of smoke and Emily and cat Larson were back in Emily's bedroom.

The Unicorn was very quick as usual and had delivered them back home, now they were safe.

Emily was happy to be back home. She started to feel tired and her eyes were ready to close.

She took off her magic dress and put it in her wardrobe. Then she jumped into bed and fell to sleep immediately as soon as her head touched the pillow.

PRINCESS PINKY AND CAT LARSON. EMILY'S SECRET VISIT TO THE WITCHES PARTY.

55

She was dreaming about the Unicorn and their magic adventures in the forest. She can see the beautiful swans in her dream and the lovely dress.

Emily could not hear in between her dreams, that the little Magic Squirrel had jumped inside her bedroom.

It approached Cat Larson and said:

"Princess Pinky sent me to check if you have arrived safe. She also asked me to pass you the Green Secret Nut. It will be your messenger between you and Princess Pinky.

However, you need to remember one thing. You can use it only once if something serious would happen to you.

Make sure, that it will be not stolen or destroyed. If Witch Wilella will find out about this she will try to take it away from you".

Cat Larson was pleased to hear this and he asked, how it would work.

"You can see the green light inside of it. It will take the signals from the human world and send them to the Castle. If you would need help, just hold the Magic Nut and tell me about it.

This nut is very special. It has grown up in the Secret Forest of the Miracles. Wilella was looking for this Nut for a very long time and she could not find it".

"Thank you for your help. You can tell Princess Pinky, that we are back home and we are safe", replied Cat Larson.

Then he hid the Secret Green Nut in a special box and placed it under Emily's bed.

"I need to think about a better place to hide it, but I can do it later. Now is a perfect time to sleep", Cat Larson jumped on Emily's bed.

He was dreaming about the Magic Castle and their trip to the Witches Party.

His paws were moving during his dreams like he was try to run away from something.

The atmosphere in the bedroom was very peaceful and calm. It was possible to hear only the sound of the wall clock, which was interfering with the silence.

PRINCESS PINKY AND CAT LARSON. EMILY'S SECRET VISIT TO THE WITCHES PARTY.

59

Emily was sleeping and cat Larson was by her feet, smiling to himself.

Suddenly, a voice from down stairs was calling up:

"Emily, time to get up. Breakfast is ready. Come on sleepy, come and eat.

You need to get ready as we are going shopping soon".

It was Emily's mum who called her little girl to wake up and to be ready in time.

Cat Larson jumped up and touched Emily's shoulder:

"Emily, your mother is calling you. Let's go downstairs for breakfast. I will tell you later, what happened while you were asleep after when we arrived".

Meanwhile, Cat Larson was thinking about where he will need to hide the Secret Green Nut.

"Well. Maybe, the cabinet with the spicy and old jars will be the best place. Nobody ever gos there too often to see what can be in that place".

Cat Larson was pleased, that he found the solution. He run back to the Emily's bedroom to hide the Magic Nut while Emily was having her breakfast.

"I need to tell Emily about this after when she finishes eating", thought Cat Larson. Then he went to the kitchen to join the family for breakfast.

He did not notice at that time, that a few pairs of sparky red eyes were watching him from the corner.

There were Wilella's spies, which she sent to Emily's house to watch Emily and Cat Larson.

The breakfast was going the pleasant and delicious way with a lot of tasty things.

Suddenly, Cat Larson heard a noise from the cabinet, just where he had hid the Secret Green Nut a few minutes ago.

He ran towards the cabinet and jumped inside. It was just in time for this action as he can see a few rats who tried to steal the Secret Nut away with them.

He jumped on one of them and pressed her to the floor with his paw. The rest of the rats just screamed and run away in lots of different directions.

PRINCESS PINKY AND CAT LARSON. EMILY'S SECRET VISIT TO THE WITCHES PARTY.

63

Unfortunately, the Secret Green Nut was lying on the floor and was broken into two pieces.

Cat Larson heard, that Emily had stepped inside the cabinet too.

"What has happened here?" asked Emily and looked at Cat Larson, then at the pieces of green nut on the floor.

"We had some visitors", he replied to her furry friend.

"Witch Wilella sent a couple of rats to us to take away from us Princess Pinky's present.

You can see it now in front of us on the floor", explained Cat Larson.

"I don't know, what is it, but can we fix it?" asked Emily.

She looked at Cat Larson with hope in her eyes and he promised her, that he will find a solution, but a little bit later.

He needed to have time to think as too many things have happened to them so suddenly.

"Let's hide it again in a special box and fix it later. I will need some help to do this from the Magic Helpers.

But I will tell you about it later", said Cat Larson.

Emily agreed with him as she always had trust her faithful friend.

She left with her mum to go shopping, Cat Larson start to think about how to deal with this tricky situation...

PRINCESS PINKY AND CAT LARSON. EMILY'S SECRET VISIT TO THE WITCHES PARTY.

65

TO BE CONTINUED...

GABRIELL MONRO

The new adventures of Emily and Cat Larson continue in the next book...

Milton Keynes UK
Ingram Content Group UK Ltd.
UKHW010712080823
426520UK00001B/59

9 798223 573579